Magic Animal Friends

For Lotte Haig-Thomas

Special thanks to Valerie Wilding

ORCHARD BOOKS

First published in Great Britain in 2016 by The Watts Publishing Group

3 5 7 9 10 8 6 4 2

A CIP catalogue record for this book is available from the British Library.

ISBN 978 1 40834 113 1

Printed in Great Britain by Clays Ltd, St Ives plc

The paper and board used in this book are made from wood from responsible sources

Orchard Books
An imprint of Hachette Children's Group
Part of The Watts Publishing Group Limited
Carmelite House, 50 Victoria Embankment, London EC4Y 0DZ

An Hachette UK Company
www.hachette.co.uk
www.hachettechildrens.co.uk

Matilda Fluffywing Helps Out

Daisy Meadows

Sunshine Meadow
Goldie's Grotto
Toadstool Cafe
Mr Cleverfeather's Inventing Shed
Toadstool Glade
Mrs Taptree's Library
Friendship Tree
Parasol Tree
Rushing Rapids
Butterfly Bowery
Entrance to the Caverns
Heart Trees
Nibblesqueak Bakery

Map of Friendship Forest

Can you keep a secret? I thought you could!
Then I'll tell you about an enchanted wood.
It lies through the door in the old oak tree,
Let's go there now - just follow me!
We'll find adventure that never ends,
And meet the Magic Animal Friends!

Love,

Goldie the Cat

Contents

CHAPTER ONE: A Bird in Need 9

CHAPTER TWO: The Sneezles 21

CHAPTER THREE: Grizelda Strikes Again 37

CHAPTER FOUR: Nasty Knitting 47

CHAPTER FIVE: Pat Shinyshell 61

CHAPTER SIX: The Colour Spy 73

CHAPTER SEVEN: Callie's Cure 83

CHAPTER EIGHT: Party Time 93

CHAPTER ONE

A Bird in Need

Jess Forester pointed to a patch of daisies at the back of her garden. "Look!" she said to her best friend, Lily Hart. "Something's moving over there!"

The two girls went to look. Hidden among the daisies was a baby sparrow, trying to flap its tiny wings.

"Oh, no," said Lily. "I think it's hurt."

Above the daisies was a tree. Jess looked up and saw a nest there. "I'm not surprised," she said. "It fell a long way."

Lily jumped to her feet. "My mum and dad will know what to do. Don't worry, little sparrow – I'm going to get help!"

She ran off and came back a couple of minutes later, followed by her dad. Mr Hart was carrying a shoebox.

"You should usually leave baby wild animals alone," said Mr Hart, as he gently lifted the sparrow into the box, "but this little bird definitely needs help."

Lily and Jess followed Mr Hart as he carried the box back across the lane. Jess ran ahead to hold open the gate to Lily's garden. There was a large barn in the garden, surrounded by hutches with rabbits, hedgehogs, piglets and a tortoise inside. This was the Helping Paw Wildlife Hospital, which was run by Lily's parents.

All the animals were injured or poorly, and Lily and Jess loved helping to care for them while they got better.

They went into the barn. Two fox cubs were scampering around a pen, trying to catch each other's bushy tails. Mrs Hart was filling up their food bowls as they squeaked and yapped. "Hello, girls!" she said. "What's in the shoebox?"

"An injured baby bird," said Lily. "Do you think it'll be OK?"

Mrs Hart gently examined the sparrow, checking its legs and wings. "Good news!" she said finally. "It's just a sprain."

"Oh, like when I twisted my ankle?" asked Jess.

"Yes! This little chap just needs to rest in the aviary for a few days," said Mrs Hart. "Pop him in a nest box, and I'll check on him later."

Lily and Jess went outside to the aviary, which was a tent made of netting. It was big enough for birds to fly around while they were getting better.

There was a young blackbird in there already, with a robin and two squawky starling chicks.

They settled the baby sparrow in a cosy nest box. It wriggled in the soft hay at the bottom, its tiny black eyes closing sleepily. "Get well soon," whispered Lily.

As they closed the door to the aviary, something caught Jess's eye. A beautiful golden cat was climbing through the hedge.

"Goldie!" Jess cried.

Goldie lived in a magical place called Friendship Forest and had taken the girls on many wonderful adventures there. Lily and Jess had made friends with lots of the forest animals, who lived in little cottages, or on boats, or even in a windmill. Best of all, the animals there could talk!

Goldie mewed, then darted away. She glanced back, mewed again, and bounded towards Brightley Stream at the bottom of the garden.

"That's strange," said Lily. "She doesn't usually run off so quickly. She must be in a hurry to go back to Friendship Forest!"

They ran after her. Goldie's fur flashed in the sunshine as she leaped over the stream's stepping stones and raced across Brightley Meadow.

"She's going so fast," said Jess, sprinting to keep up. "Grizelda must be up to something!"

Grizelda was a horrible witch who was always trying to take over Friendship Forest. Recently she had been training four young apprentice witches to help her destroy the magical Heart Trees that the animals turned to whenever they

needed help. She wanted the forest to become such a miserable place that all the animals would have to leave.

Goldie raced towards a dead-looking tree in the middle of the meadow.

The Friendship Tree!

As she reached it, it sprang to life. Green leaves unfurled on its branches and golden daffodils appeared by its trunk.

The girls reached the tree, bending over to catch their breath. Goldie mewed anxiously.

"Poor Goldie," said Jess, "she must be really worried!"

Quickly, the girls joined hands and read out loud the two words that were written in the bark.

"Friendship Forest!"

A door with a leaf-shaped handle appeared in the tree's trunk.

Lily opened it and Goldie immediately leaped into the golden light.

Jess and Lily hurried after her. Instantly,

they tingled all over, and knew they were shrinking, just a little.

As the magical glow faded, they found themselves in a beautiful, sun-dappled forest glade. Goldie was now standing upright, as tall as their shoulders, and wearing her golden scarf. Her tail twitched with concern.

The girls held her paws.

"What is it, Goldie?" asked Lily, anxiously.

"Has Grizelda done something?" added Jess.

Goldie shook her head. "No, it's something else," she said. "One of the animals needs your help. Let's hurry!"

CHAPTER TWO

The Sneezles

Lily and Jess raced after Goldie, past the Twinkletail mouse family's cottage and the Toadstool Café, where the Slipperslide family of otters were sitting outside eating hazelnut cupcakes. There was no time to chat to their friends, so the girls just waved and hurried on.

At last Goldie stopped by a strange round building, that looked like a huge nest, up in a tree. It was made of many branches woven together, each covered with bright blue and yellow flowers.

A sign above the door said, 'Get Well Grove'.

"The Fluffywing family live here," Goldie explained. "Mr and Mrs Fluffywing are both doctors. They care for all the forest animals."

She jingled the feather-shaped doorbell.

They heard an excited squawk, and a door above them burst open.

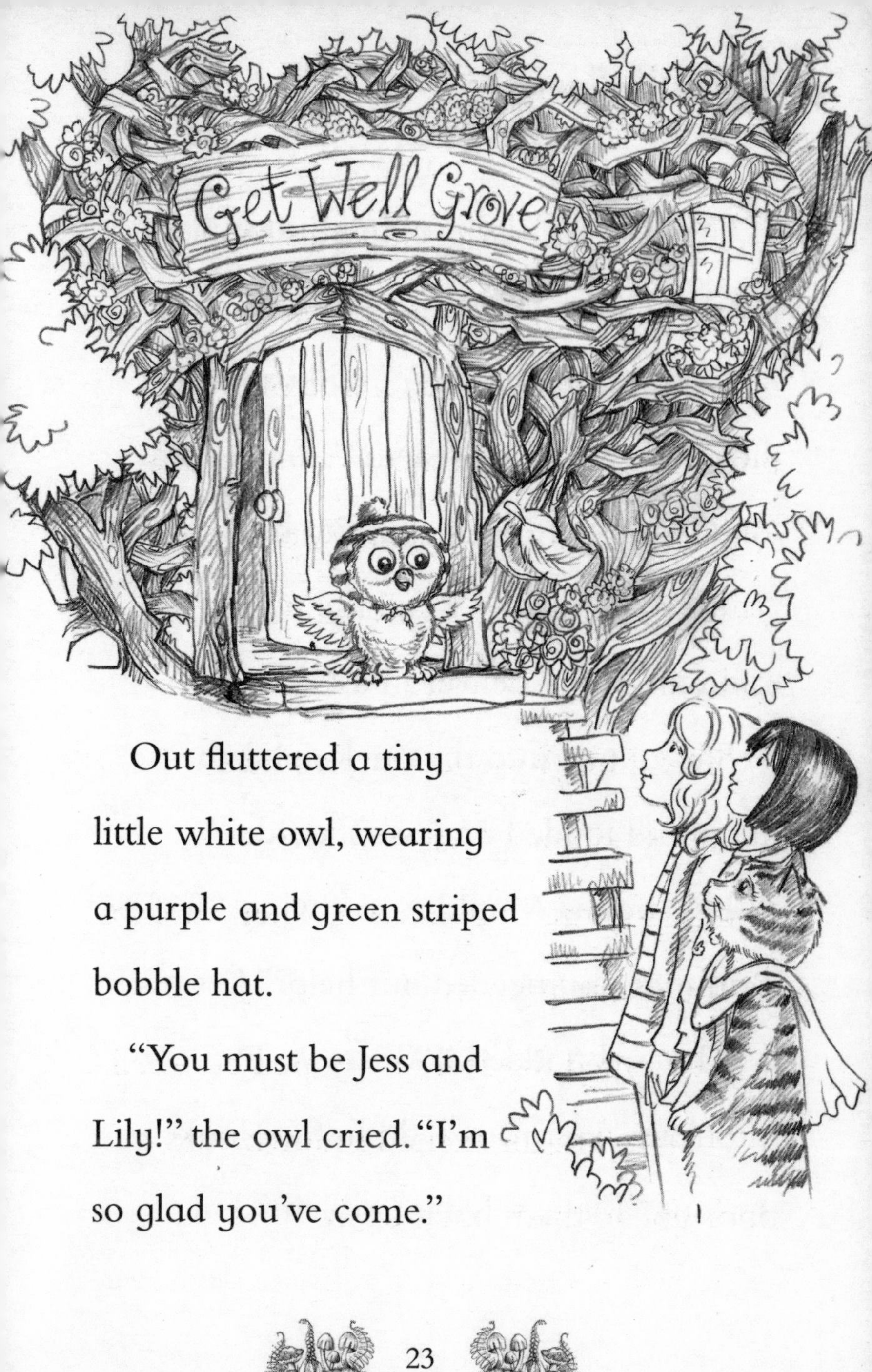

Out fluttered a tiny little white owl, wearing a purple and green striped bobble hat.

"You must be Jess and Lily!" the owl cried. "I'm so glad you've come."

"Yes we are," Lily said with a smile. "What's your name?"

"Matilda Fluffywing," said the owl, hovering in front of them. "I help Mum and Dad," she added, fluffing her feathers. "I carry medicines to all the poorly animals in my delivery basket."

She zipped into the air, looped-the-loop and landed on Jess's shoulder.

Jess stroked Matilda's soft wing. "Goldie said that you needed our help?" Jess asked.

The owl nodded. "We've got a problem." Her round, fluffy face looked serious. "I love solving problems, but

I can't solve this one. Goldie told us about Helping Paw Hospital, and we thought you might be able to help."

"We'll do our best," Lily said, with a smile. "What's wrong?"

"We've got a patient and we don't know what's the matter with her," said Matilda. She fluttered back up to the door. "Come on in."

Goldie hurried up some wooden steps to the house, and the girls followed after her. The door was low, so they had to duck to go through it, but once they were inside they could stand upright.

They were in a round room lined with shelves. Each was crammed with bottles filled with flowers, jars holding wisps of colourful smoke, a heap of bandages made of grass, and a pile of cobwebs labelled, 'For cuts and scratches'. The shelves covered the walls from floor to ceiling, the bottles and jars glittering in the sunlight that shone through a window in the ceiling.

"Wow," breathed Jess.

Lily read out the label on a glass jar. *"Jellyberry Ointment For Tickly Whiskers."*

"Starflower Soothing Cream For Ruffled Feathers," Jess read from a little wooden pot.

"Primrose Petals For Poorly Paws," said Lily, pointing to a large box.

They followed Matilda as she flew into an airy room. Two grown-up owls were sitting at a table, mixing medicines.

Nearby were three little beds. One had pretty flowered curtains drawn around it.

A strange sound came from behind the curtains. *Choo!*

"Mum, Dad!" said Matilda. "Goldie has brought Jess and Lily to help us."

Choo! The sound came again from behind the curtains.

The two owls jumped up. "Welcome, welcome!" said Matilda's dad, who had a pair of small round glasses balanced on the end of his beak. "I'm Doctor Fluffywing."

Choo!

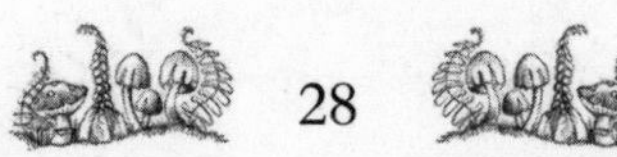

"And I'm called Doctor Fluffywing too," said Matilda's mum as she hugged the girls. "Thank you for coming." She picked up a bamboo tube. "I'm going to listen to our patient's breathing with the Chest Checker. Our cousin, Mr Cleverfeather, invented it. Come and see."

Jess, Lily and Goldie followed her behind the flowery curtains.

Choo!

The patient was a small brown mouse, wearing a necklace of pink rosebuds. She was tucked up in bed. Her whiskers were drooping and her tiny nose looked sore.

"Callie Twinkletail!" said Lily. She and Jess had met Callie when they'd helped her sister, Molly, on one of their earliest adventures in Friendship Forest.

"Poor you," said Jess, gently patting the little mouse's tiny paw. "What's wrong?"

"*Choo!*" Callie sneezed, making the funny sound they'd heard earlier.

"That's the problem," said Matilda.

"Callie has the sneezles, and we can't stop them."

"*Choo!*" Callie's ears quivered with every sneeze.

"We've tried Candyfloss Cough Mixture and our Special Sniffle Soother," said Matilda's mum, "but nothing helps."

"Perhaps Callie has hayfever," Jess suggested. "My dad has it and pollen makes him sneeze. Maybe Callie's allergic to her necklace," she said, pointing to the rosebuds.

"*Choo!* I'm not," said Callie. "I pick – *choo!* – roses every – *choo!* – week to

make a new necklace. They never give me sneezles. *Choo! Choo, choo, CHOO!*"

"Could you have caught a cold? asked Lily. "Have you been splashing in any puddles recently?"

"No," said Callie. "*Choo!* I hate – *choo!* – getting my – *choo!* – paws wet."

"Poor Callie," said Matilda's dad. "We really must find a cure!"

Jess turned to Goldie. "Do you think one of the Heart Trees could help?"

Goldie's ears pricked up. "That's a great idea! We could go to the Kindness Tree. It always knows how to help."

Then she gave a little frown. "I just hope Grizelda hasn't done anything to harm it…"

Grizelda had already attacked three of the Heart Trees in the forest – the Memory Tree, the Laughter Tree and the Sweet Dreams Tree. But the girls and Goldie had stopped her wicked spells. They had even persuaded three of her trainee witches to be good.

"We'll stop her if she has," said Jess fiercely. "What does the Kindness Tree do, Goldie?"

"It brings kindness to the forest," Goldie explained, "and it helps the animals do kind deeds."

"How does it do that?" Lily asked.

"You know how Friendship Forest animals love being kind and doing things for others?" said Goldie. "Well, sometimes they're not sure how."

"Like when Tipper Taptree the woodpecker was sad," said Matilda, flying up and down excitedly.

"I didn't know how to cheer him up, so I asked the Kindness Tree. It gave me the idea to bake him some chestnut cakes."

"Making Callie better would be kind," said Goldie.

"*Choo!* It really – *choo!* – would," said Callie. She gave a sad sniff and rubbed her eyes.

Lily stroked the mouse's soft fur. "We'll work out what's wrong," she said. "Don't worry."

"Can I go to the Kindness Tree too?" asked Matilda, fluttering excitedly around the room. "Please, Mum? Please, Dad?"

Both Doctor Fluffywings nodded. "We must try anything to help our patients," said her mum. "Off you go! And good luck!"

"Come on!" said Matilda, fluttering to the door. "Let's go!"

CHAPTER THREE

Grizelda Strikes Again

Lily, Jess and Goldie hurried through the forest, following the heart-shaped path that linked the four Heart Trees. Matilda fluttered over their heads.

After a little while they reached a tree with pink, heart-shaped leaves. Its slender branches were covered in pale green moss

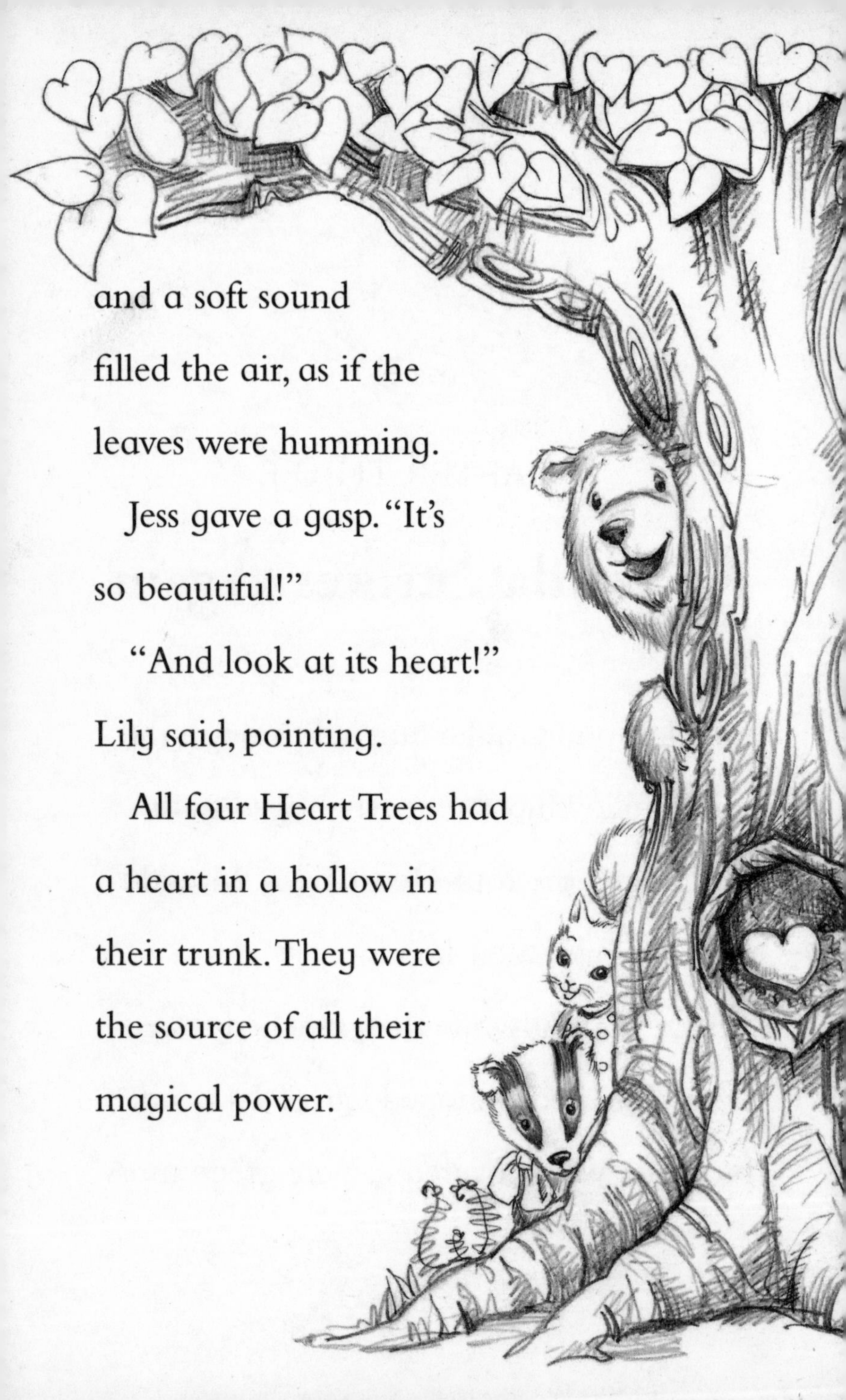

and a soft sound filled the air, as if the leaves were humming.

Jess gave a gasp. "It's so beautiful!"

"And look at its heart!" Lily said, pointing.

All four Heart Trees had a heart in a hollow in their trunk. They were the source of all their magical power.

The Kindness Tree's heart was as soft and pink as a rose petal.

Everyone was gazing at the heart when the bushes surrounding the tree rustled suddenly, making the girls jump.

Out came Great-Uncle Greybear, Sophie and Woody Flufftail the squirrels, Lottie Littlestripe the badger, Emily Prickleback the hedgehog and lots of other animals.

"Hello!" Jess said, surprised. "What are you doing here?"

"We're protecting the Kindness Tree," said Emily, adjusting her tiara. "Grizelda's already attacked the other Heart Trees, so we're not letting her harm this one."

Sophie swished her bushy tail. "Kindness is far too important to Friendship Forest," she said.

The animals linked paws and made a circle around the tree.

"You're all very brave," Lily said.

Goldie explained that they'd come to ask the tree for help. "One of us must pick a leaf," she told Matilda and the girls, "and gaze deep into the tree's heart.

It will show us how to help Callie."

"You pick the leaf, Matilda," said Lily.

The little owl flew up. "They're so lovely and soft!" she said as she fluttered among the leaves.

"You're getting covered in them, Matilda!" Lily giggled. Pink leaves were sticking to the little owl's feathers and her woolly hat.

But Jess had spotted two orbs of light flying towards them. One was a familiar yellow-green and the other was blue.

"Look out! It's Grizelda and one of her young witches!" she yelled.

The frightened animals huddled behind Great-Uncle Greybear as the two orbs burst in showers of smelly sparks.

There stood Grizelda in her purple tunic and tight trousers over long, pointed black boots. Her green hair coiled and

wiggled around her head like snakes.

Beside her was Ivy, the last of the four apprentice witches who were helping her. She was about the same age as Lily and Jess, and had long, twisty hair with blue streaks. A large blue spider sat grinning on her shoulder. His legs were a blur as he spun a thread of cobweb.

"Ha-de-ha!" Ivy giggled. "Your legs tickle, Sidney!"

"Quiet!" Grizelda snapped. She strode around the animals. "What do you think you're doing?" she asked them.

Great-Uncle Greybear held out his arms, shielding the smaller animals. "We won't let you harm the Kindness Tree, Grizelda," he said.

"He's right!" Jess shouted.

"Ha haa!" the witch shrieked. "You won't stop my plan this time. I've saved my most powerful spell until last!" She pointed at Ivy. "And my most powerful apprentice, too!"

She pointed towards the sky and chanted:

"This spell you meddling girls won't fix.
I'll stop your interfering tricks.
Magic lightning, strike the tree!
You cannot mend what you can't see!"

A bolt of lightning burst out of the sky and hit the tree. Jess and Lily spluttered as stinking, green smoke filled the air.

When the smoke cleared, the horrified girls gasped. All that was left of the Kindness Tree was a heap of ash.

"Oh no!" cried Goldie. "Without the tree, there won't be any more kindness in the forest!"

CHAPTER FOUR

Nasty Knitting

Grizelda threw her head back, cackling. "Try fixing that, girlies!" she screeched. "All those soppy animals won't be helping each other any more! Kindness has left the forest, so they'll want to leave, too!"

Ivy smirked at them, her hands on her hips. "So there!"

Grizelda's snaking hair squirmed wildly around her head. "Friendship Forest will soon be mine! Ivy will stop you from meddling in my plan!"

And with a snap of her fingers, and another spitting shower of smelly sparks, she vanished.

The girls comforted the trembling animals. Jess cuddled Lottie Littlestripe and stroked Sophie's soft fur. Woody Flufftail climbed onto Lily's lap, curling his tail over his eyes. All the other animals leaned against the girls, clutching them with quivering paws. Matilda huddled next to Goldie, while Great-Uncle Greybear poked the ash that used to be the Kindness Tree.

Not far away, Ivy sat in a wild strawberry patch and pulled out two knitting needles from her cloak. Sidney was on her shoulder, spinning a long thread of cobweb. Ivy wound it onto her needles and began to knit.

"What are we going to do?" Goldie said miserably.

Matilda's eyes opened wide. "It's a difficult problem to solve," she said, "but we'll try, won't we? If we don't get the Kindness Tree back, Friendship Forest won't be a nice place to live any more."

Lily stroked her soft feathers. Most of the leaves that had stuck to Matilda had fallen off, but there were still some on her hat. "Of course we'll try." She sighed. "Though I don't know how."

"I do!" said Jess. "Great-Uncle Greybear's scrapbook helped us fix the

other Heart Trees."

She turned to the big elderly bear. "Could we borrow it again, please?"

"Of course," he replied in his gruffly voice. He fished in his picnic basket and pulled out the scrapbook. "I brought it along with me, just in case."

The animals gathered around. The book's golden pages gleamed.

"It's so shiny!" said Emily Prickleback.

"That's thanks to Dandelion, one of the young witches!" Lily explained. "She tried to stop us using the book, but she just made it prettier!"

Goldie and the girls carefully read every page in the book. Finally, Lily closed it. "There's nothing about what to do if a Heart Tree's completely destroyed," she said sadly.

Matilda rubbed the top of her bobble hat with one wing. "There's always a way to solve a problem, isn't there?" she chirped, then fluttered over to Great-Uncle Greybear.

"Where did the Heart Trees come from?" Lily asked.

"I don't know," he replied. "I was just a fluffy little cub then, more interested in honey and milk than trees."

Suddenly Woody Flufftail the squirrel squealed. "Look out!"

Jess glanced up. A shiny net whizzed through the air and landed on her head.

"Yuck!" she cried, pulling at it. "A sticky spider's web!"

She looked over to where Ivy sat in the strawberry patch, knitting so fast that her needles were a blur.

"Ivy's knitting them!" Jess cried.

"Ha-de-ha!" Ivy said, flinging another knitted web at Goldie. "My magic makes these webs super-sticky!"

Sidney laughed too, and passed another long strand of cobweb to Ivy.

Jess peeled the sticky web off Goldie's ears. Emily and Sophie ducked as Ivy threw more webs at them. Ivy and her spider giggled again.

"Ha-de-ha! Grizelda wants Sidney and me to stay right here," said Ivy. "So there! We won't let you fix the Kindness Tree."

"If only we could," Jess muttered gloomily.

They all huddled behind a tree, away from Ivy's sticky webs.

Great-Uncle Greybear scratched his furry chin. "Young Matilda has got me thinking about where the Heart Trees came from," he said. "There's someone who might know. He's almost as old as me, and he collects interesting facts about trees and flowers."

"Who?" everybody asked.

But suddenly Great-Uncle Greybear scowled. "I don't want to tell you," he said, crossing his paws over his chest.

The girls, Goldie and the other animals gasped.

Then Great-Uncle Greybear shook his big furry head in confusion. "I'm so sorry, young bears," he said. "I don't know what came over me. I didn't mean to be horrible."

Jess patted his shoulder. "It's all right," she said. "It must be because the Kindness Tree has gone."

Lily nodded. "It's not your fault. We know you'd never usually be unkind."

"Oh, we must put the kindness back in the forest!" Great-Uncle Greybear sighed. "My friend who can help is Pat Shinyshell the tortoise."

"That's great!" cried Goldie. "Where can we find him?"

But the elderly bear looked worried. "Pat takes long walks around

the forest every day. He might be difficult to find."

"We'll just have to try," said Jess. "It's our only chance!"

Great-Uncle Greybear and the other animals wished the four friends luck as they set off through the forest.

Lily glanced around at the ferns and bushes. "It's going to be very hard to spot Pat," she said anxiously.

"I can solve that problem!" said Matilda, happily. "I'll fly up as high as I can. I'll be able to see the whole forest from up there!"

The little owl soared upwards, while Jess, Lily and Goldie searched for Pat on foot. They'd only been walking for a minute when Matilda screeched and dived towards them.

"What is it?" called Jess. "Have you found him already?"

But Matilda was flapping and squawking in alarm. "Smoke!" she cried. "Smoke in the forest! Something's burning!"

Sure enough, grey clouds of smoke billowed through the trees ahead.

"Hurry!" Goldie shouted, racing towards the smoke. "Somebody needs our help!"

CHAPTER FIVE

Pat Shinyshell

Lily and Jess ran after Goldie, while Matilda zoomed ahead of them, her fluffy little wings a blur.

"The smoke's coming from the Nibblesqueak Bakery!" she squawked.

"Those poor hamsters!" cried Jess.

They dashed through the trees and

into the clearing where the little bakery stood. Smoke was streaming from one of the windows, but to their relief, Mr and Mrs Nibblesqueak and all the little Nibblesqueaks were outside.

"Is everyone OK?" Lily asked anxiously.

"Yes," Olivia Nibblesqueak said in a small, shaky voice.

"We're fine," said Mr Nibblesqueak. "But I'm afraid our cakes are all burned."

"Hoot! Hoot!" came from above them.

With a flurry of feathers, Mr Cleverfeather the owl landed beside them, holding one of his inventions.

Lily thought it was like a fat round helicopter with letters on the outside.

"Hello, Cousin Matilda!" he said, then waved at the invention. "I saw smoke, so I brought my Flitter Flutter Spray."

"Flitter Flutter spray?" asked Lily.

"It flitter-flutters around and sprays water," the owl explained.

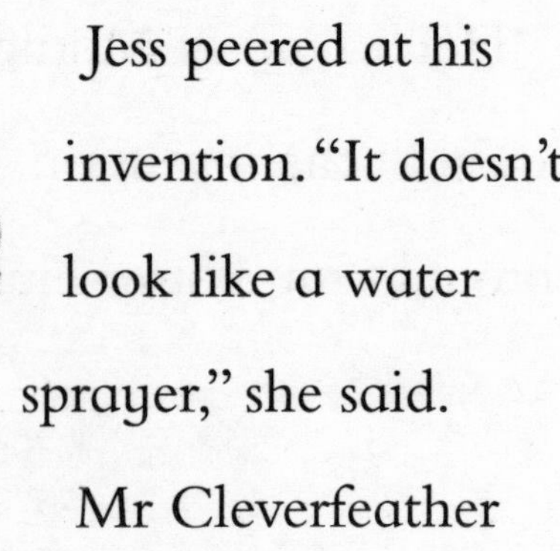

Jess peered at his invention. "It doesn't look like a water sprayer," she said.

Mr Cleverfeather glanced down. "Bother!" he said. "I've brought my Colour Spy by mistake. It searches for different colours. I am a billy sird," he added, muddling his words as usual.

"You're not silly," Jess said gently. "Anyway, it doesn't matter, there's no fire. It's just smoke from the oven."

"Our cakes are all ruined," wailed little Penny Nibblesqueak.

"And they were for a special birthday surprise." Olivia said miserably.

"We can't have a birthday without cake!" Mrs Nibblesqueak cried.

"I can't help with cakes," Mr Cleverfeather said crossly. He waved a wing and flew away.

Goldie, Jess and Lily exchanged worried glances.

"First Great-Uncle Greybear was mean," said Goldie, "then the surprise cakes and Mr Cleverfeather's helpful plan went wrong."

"It's all because Grizelda destroyed the Kindness Tree," said Jess. "It's making the animals mean – and if they do try to be kind, it doesn't work."

Matilda gave a gasp of worry. "But fixing the Kindness Tree *is* kind. Does that mean we won't be able to do it?"

Lily picked her up and cradled her in her arms. "That leaf tucked in your bobble hat is a little bit of the Kindness

Tree," she said, "so you're protected from the magic being gone. We know that from when we saved the other Heart Trees."

"We're protected, too," said Jess, "because we're from the human world."

"And I was once a stray in their world," said Goldie, "so I'm all right. But we have to find Pat Shinyshell before kindness is lost from the forest forever!"

"Ooh!" said Olivia Nibblesqueak, who was still close by. "Pat Shinyshell walked by here a little while ago on his way to pick gooseberries on Gooseberry Green, I saw him!"

"Which way is Gooseberry Green?" asked Lily excitedly.

But Olivia stuck out her tongue. "I'm not telling," she said. Then she gave herself a shake. "I'm sorry! I didn't mean to be unkind." She pointed towards a path by a patch of daisies. "It's that way."

As they set off, Jess noticed Mr Cleverfeather had left his Colour Spy behind.

"We'd better look after this," she said, picking it up.

They set off for Gooseberry Green, with Matilda flying overhead. Before long they

were in a field of prickly bushes, laden with plump gooseberries. As the girls and Goldie started searching for Pat, Matilda gave a squawk.

"Here!" she cried.

They ran to where Matilda had landed beside an elderly tortoise. He wore a little red top hat, and had two big bags of gooseberries balanced on his shell.

"I'm de...light...ed to meet you," Pat said slowly. A bag slipped off his shell. "Oh, dear," he said.

"We'll help," said Jess.

The friends each took one of his bags.

"You're very...kind," said Pat. "My log cabin's...this-a-way."

Slowly, they followed Pat to his home beside a flower-filled meadow.

The log cabin was long and low and its arched entrance was just the right shape for Pat to pass through. The girls couldn't get inside, so they stacked Pat's bags in the doorway.

"Would you like some...lettuce tea?" Pat asked slowly.

"Er, no thanks," said Jess, imagining how long it would take the tortoise to make it. "We do need help, though."

The girls explained all about the Kindness Tree.

"Great-Uncle Greybear thought you might know what to do," said Lily.

"Hmm," said Pat. "Let me…think." He closed his eyes.

Pat was still for so long the girls thought he'd fallen asleep, but then he opened his eyes and spoke.

"You can't do anything about…that tree. But you could…grow a new one."

They all gasped. "A new Kindness Tree!" cried Lily. "But how?"

CHAPTER SIX

The Colour Spy

The four friends fidgeted as Pat Shinyshell slowly explained what to do.

"First," he said, "find a Heart Tree seedling. They're…very rare. But if there is one…my meadow is where it will be."

"Great!" said Jess, leaping up. "What do they look like?"

Pat closed his eyes.

Lily and Jess hopped from foot to foot, desperate to hear his reply.

Finally he opened his eyes and spoke. "They have...heart-shaped leaves..."

Lily, Matilda, Goldie and Jess were about to head for the meadow, when Pat said, "And..."

They waited.

"If you want to turn a Heart Tree seedling...into a Kindness Tree," said Pat, "you must...surround it with kindness. If no one finds Heart Tree seedlings, they become...normal trees."

He stared at them.

"What are you…waiting for?"

"Thanks, Pat!" they said, and dashed into the meadow.

"Be careful!" cried Lily. "Don't trample on a seedling by mistake!"

Pat followed slowly behind them.

Goldie gazed at the mass of colourful flowers. "How can we find the right seedling in all this?" she gasped.

"I know!" said Jess, darting back to Pat. "What colour are the seedling's leaves?" she asked.

"They're…pink," said Pat.

Jess held up Mr Cleverfeather's Colour Spy and pressed four buttons: P I N K.

"If there's a pink seedling here," she said, "this should find it!" She pressed 'GO', and the Colour Spy rose up and floated across the meadow. It had just passed Pat, when it went *beep*!

The girls reached it first. Lily bent to see what the Colour Spy had found. "Oh!" she said. "It's only a rosebud."

She leaned over to sniff it, but Pat said, "Stop!" He blinked slowly. "That's not… a rose."

"Isn't it?" Jess said, as Matilda flew down to see what was happening.

"It's sneezeweed," he said. "Don't pick—"

But it was too late. Matilda had already picked it.

"*A-a-a-chooo!*" she sneezed. "*A-a-a-chooo!*"

Pat trudged to a purple flower with leaves like green spikes. "Here, Matilda," he said, "sniff this... Cool-and-Calm Crocus."

Matilda did as he said, and the sneezing stopped.

"Phew!" she said. Then she stared at the Cool-and-Calm Crocus, and hooted in excitement. "We can solve Callie's sneezles problem after all! We just need to give her one of these to sniff!"

"Yes!" said Lily. "She must have made her necklace out of sneezeweeds, thinking they were roses! We can cure her!"

"Hooray!" the others cheered.

A moment or so later, Pat cheered, too.

"That's Callie's problem solved," said Lily, "but we've still got to find a Heart Tree seedling or there'll be no more kindness in the forest. Set the Colour Spy off again, Jess."

This time, the Colour Spy went *beep* before it was halfway across the meadow!

They chased after it. There, glowing pink in the sunshine, was a tiny Heart Tree seedling. It had a pair of pink heart-shaped leaves, and almost reached the girls' ankles.

The friends cheered again.

Pat came over. "I'll fetch a plant...pot."

"Um, shall I get it?" Lily asked, thinking how long it would take Pat to go all the way there and back.

"There's one...by the back door," said Pat, and off Lily went.

Lily returned with the pot and a little garden fork, and Jess carefully dug up the seedling and potted it. Matilda picked a fresh Cool-and-Calm Crocus for Callie.

"Thanks for your help, Pat," said Lily.

"I'll come and help you next time you need gooseberries," Matilda said.

As soon as she'd spoken, Jess gave a yell. "Look at the seedling!"

The baby tree was growing! It grew until it reached Jess's knees and new heart-shaped leaves burst out from lots of new branches.

Matilda stared at the tiny tree in amazement. "What happened?"

"You were kind...to me," said Pat, "so it's growing into a Kindness Tree... already. Everyone just needs to keep doing...kind deeds."

They set off, smiling happily.

"We can put kindness back into Friendship Forest now," said Jess.

Lily nodded. "And I've got an idea for another kind deed – helping the Nibblesqueaks at their bakery!"

CHAPTER SEVEN

Callie's Cure

A little later, Goldie, Matilda and the girls stood around the Nibblesqueaks' kitchen table. They were covered in blobs of icing, and grinning from ear to ear.

"It's amazing!" said Mrs Nibblesqueak as she looked at the new cake. "How did you do it?"

"First," said Lily, "we cut the burnt bits off all the little cakes."

"Olivia made some icing," said Jess.

"Then," said Matilda, "we used the icing to stick bits of cake together."

"And we nibbled the burnt bits of cake," said Lily with a chuckle.

"Finally," said Goldie, "we decorated it with more icing!"

"There'll be a surprise birthday cake after all!" Olivia's mum said happily. "You're so kind."

Goldie smiled. "Real kindness is doing something nice for someone, even if it doesn't go perfectly."

"Well, the cake looks perfect," said Mr Nibblesqueak.

"And the seedling's growing again," Matilda shouted. "It's as tall as Jess!"

Little branches curled out from the main stem. More leaves sprouted and opened as the friends watched.

"It's so tall that I think we need to do

just one more kind deed before we plant it," said Goldie. "We'd better go!"

The Nibblesqueaks said goodbye, and the others set off.

As soon as the friends reached Get Well Grove they heard, "*Choo! CHOO!*"

Matilda grinned and flew inside, Goldie and the girls following her up the steps.

"We've solved Callie's problem!" Matilda told her parents.

"How?" asked her dad. "We still don't even know what has caused her sneezles!"

Matilda laughed. "We do! She picked sneezeweeds instead of roses!"

She took the Cool-and-Calm Crocus to Callie's bed. "Sniff this," she said.

"*Choo!*" Callie sneezed. She sat up and sniffed the flower.

Her eyes widened.

Her ears stood up.

She smiled. "The sneezles have stopped!" She took off her necklace of pink flowers.

"Thank you, everybody. I'll never pick sneezeweeds again!"

Matilda hugged her. "I'm glad we solved your problem!" she said.

Jess grinned and pointed through the window. "And we've solved another one!"

The seedling had grown even taller than the girls. It had bark on its trunk, and it was covered with beautiful pink heart-shaped leaves.

"Thanks to everyone's kind deeds," said Goldie, "it's not a seedling any more. It's a true Heart Tree!"

Lily lifted Callie up so she could see it.

"Let's take it back to where the old Kindness Tree grew," said Jess.

Goldie and Matilda led the way to the heart-shaped path, while Lily and Jess followed, carrying the tree between them. When they reached the clearing where the Kindness Tree used to be, they were greeted by a chorus of cheers from Great-Uncle Greybear, Emily Prickleback, Sophie Flufftail and all the other animals.

Lottie Littlestripe, the badger cub, started digging a hole for the new tree.

"Now, let's get the tree planted!" said Lily. She, Jess and Goldie picked it up.

Suddenly, Goldie whispered, "Look!"

She pointed at the nearest tree.

Jess gasped. “It’s Ivy and Sidney!”

“You’ve got a new Kindness Tree!” Ivy said in amazement. Then she shook her head. “Never mind – I’ll get rid of it.”

Clack, clack, clack went Ivy's needles as she knitted more webs.

"Watch out!" yelled Jess as Ivy flung the webs. They moved the Kindness Tree out of the way just in time and the webs sailed over the top of it.

"We'll never get the tree planted at this rate!" said Goldie, her tail twitching with worry. "There won't be any more kindness in the forest after all!"

Ivy laughed at her. "Ha-de-ha!"

But Sidney giggled so much he fell out of the tree. He lay on his back, wriggling his legs. "Ow-ow-ow!" he cried.

Ivy jumped down and burst into tears. "He's hurt!" she wailed.

"Oh, no!" cried Jess.

The girls ran to help him. He was holding one of his feet. "It's probably only a sprain," said Lily. "Matilda, what do you think?"

Matilda came over to Sidney. "There, there. Hold still, please." She felt his poorly leg with her feathered wing. "Lily's right," she said. "It's a sprain. But I've just the thing back at the Get Well Grotto. Don't worry, Sidney! We'll make you better!"

CHAPTER EIGHT

Party Time!

Matilda was soon back. She dropped her delivery basket in Lily's lap. Inside was a bottle of ointment with yellow swirls in it.

"Daisy-Chain Sprain Cream," Lily read.

She opened it, and Matilda patted the cream onto Sidney's leg, then wrapped it in a leaf bandage.

Sidney wiggled his leg. "It feels better already," he said. "Thanks, Matilda."

Ivy darted to Matilda and gave her a kiss on her feathery head. "You've been so kind to Sidney and me," she said, "even though we were mean to you."

As Ivy settled Sidney on her shoulder, the Heart Tree rustled and shimmered. With a flash of dazzling sparkles, it vanished, then reappeared in the hole the animals had dug.

"It's the final bit of kindness the tree needed!" said Goldie.

Everyone stared in wonder as another stream of magical sparkles swirled around the tree. Its branches grew longer, the trunk grew broader, and leaves uncurled.

"It's just as big as the old Kindness Tree was," Jess said in wonder.

The sparkles drifted down to gather around a hollow in the trunk. When they cleared, a new beautiful pink heart was nestled inside.

"We've done it!" whispered Matilda, flying a loop-the-loop in delight.

Ivy and Sidney stood, open-mouthed, as the animals and girls gave a cheer.

But a yellow-green orb of light was floating towards them.

Jess groaned. "It's Grizelda!"

The witch appeared in a burst of sparks. "You meddling girls have ruined my plan again!" She turned her face to Ivy. "You're useless at being horrible," she snarled. "You have a lot to learn!"

"Ha-de-ha!" Ivy laughed. "Actually, me and Sidney have learned a lot already. We've learned that it's better to be kind, so we're not helping you any more."

She put her hands on her hips and stuck out her chin. Together, she and Sidney said, "So there!"

Before Grizelda could reply, three more orbs of light darted towards them: one green, another purple and the third yellow.

They burst into sparks. There stood the three other trainee witches, Nettle, Dandelion and Thistle.

"Hi, everyone!" Nettle smiled, patting her spiky green hair.

Thistle waved her broomstick. "Hello!"

"Hello-wello!" said Dandelion.

"What do you lot want?" Grizelda screeched.

Dandelion pulled out a potion bottle from her pocket and grinned. "We're going to make a spell to stop you harming the Heart Trees ever again," she said. "Then we'll train to be good witches instead of horrible ones like you!"

"And you won't stop us," said Ivy.

All four witches put their hands on their hips, stuck out their chins and said, "SO THERE!"

Grizelda's face went purple. "This isn't the last you'll see of me," she snarled.

She snapped her fingers and disappeared in a burst of stinky sparks.

The four witches, the girls and all their animal friends gave a cheer that rang through the forest.

"Hooray! We've saved the Heart Trees!"

Later that afternoon, the girls went to Toadstool Glade for a birthday party.

The Longwhiskers rabbit family had hung a banner across the front of the Toadstool Café. It said "Happy 101st birthday, Great-Uncle Greybear!"

Jess grinned. "Now we know who the surprise cake was for!"

The four friends gave the birthday bear a huge hug.

"Thank you," he said. "And a little bird called Matilda tells me I should thank you for my birthday cake, too!"

"Tea time!" Mrs Nibblesqueak called. All their friends gathered around to share the cake and other tasty treats.

Lily grinned happily. "Everyone's being kind again," she said.

"And their kind deeds are working," added Jess.

"Thanks to you two," said Goldie.

"And me!" said Matilda.

"Especially you!" said Jess.

"I'm afraid it's time for Lily and Jess to go home now," Goldie said.

Matilda gave them the Daisy Chain Sprain Cream. "Would you like this for your hospital?" she said shyly.

"Thanks!" said Lily.

They each planted a birthday kiss on Great-Uncle Greybear's cheek, and said goodbye to their friends, with special hugs for the four small witches.

"Don't worry about the Heart Trees," Ivy told them. "Our new spell will protect them for ever."

"Brilliant!" said Jess.

"Goodbye," everyone called as they left. "Come back soon!"

When they reached the Friendship Tree, Goldie touched a paw to the trunk, and a door appeared.

Lily opened it, letting golden light shine out. "Come and get us as soon as Grizelda causes trouble again," she said.

Goldie smiled. "Of course! Friendship Forest will always need you!"

Lily and Jess hugged her before stepping into the golden glow. They felt the familiar tingle that meant that they were growing back to their normal size.

When the light cleared, they were home in Brightley Meadow.

"What a wonderful adventure!" said Jess as they ran back to Helping Paw.

"It was amazing!" Lily agreed. "I can't wait to go back to Friendship Forest again!" She held up the Daisy Chain Sprain Cream. "Now let's do something kind for the little baby sparrow!"

The End

Maisie Dappletrot is the smallest pony in Friendship Forest. But when wicked witch Grizelda arrives with three fearsome unicorns, Maisie shows she's a little horse with a big heart!

Find out more in the next adventure,

Maisie Dappletrot Saves the Day

Turn over for a sneak peek ...

The girls followed Goldie to the side of the cottage, where three carts were lined up. There was a big blue one, a big yellow one and a small red one.

"It is a stable, isn't it?" cried Jess. "Does a horse family live here?"

As soon as she'd spoken, they heard the clackety sound of hooves. From the back of the cottage trotted a pretty grey and white Shetland pony, pulling a cart.

The girls grinned in delight as they recognised her from their adventure with Mia Floppyear the bunny.

"Hello, Mrs Dappletrot!" cried Lily.

"Why, hello, girls!" Mrs Dappletrot called. "Welcome to our home!"

Jess tugged Lily's sleeve and pointed at Mrs Dappletrot's cart. Lily gasped out loud as she saw it – it was a pile of sparkling jewels that glittered in the sun!

Read

Maisie Dappletrot Saves the Day

to find out what happens next!

Magic Animal Friends

Can Jess and Lily stop Grizelda and her young witches from ruining the Heart Trees? Read all the books in series four to find out!

COMING SOON!
Look out for
Jess and Lily's
next adventure:
Maisie Dappletrot
Saves the Day!

www.magicanimalfriends.com

Puzzle Fun!

Can you spot the five differences between the two pictures of Matilda Fluffywing's parents?

Answers: 1. Straw in cup 2. Label on bottle, middle shelf 3. Bottle, middle shelf 4. Glasses on owl 5. Black label on bottle

Jess and Lily's Animal Facts

Lily and Jess love lots of different animals – both in Friendship Forest and in the real world.

Here are their top facts about

OWLS

like Matilda Fluffywing:

- There are about 200 different species of owl. The smallest is the Elf Owl.
- Owls do not have teeth so they swallow their food whole.
- Owls can fly silently, which means they are very good at hunting and catching food.
- A group of owls is called a 'parliament'.

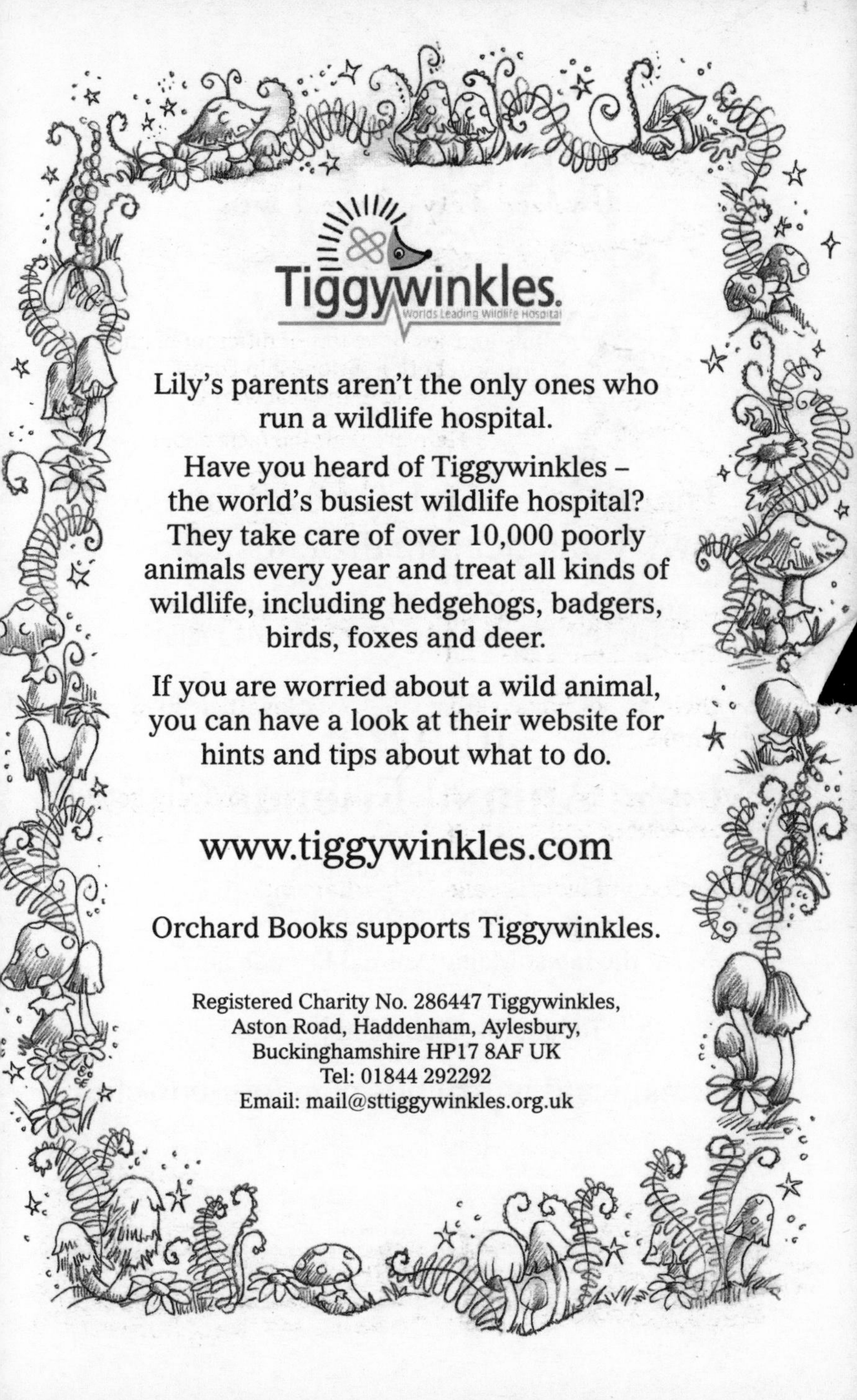

Lily's parents aren't the only ones who run a wildlife hospital.

Have you heard of Tiggywinkles – the world's busiest wildlife hospital? They take care of over 10,000 poorly animals every year and treat all kinds of wildlife, including hedgehogs, badgers, birds, foxes and deer.

If you are worried about a wild animal, you can have a look at their website for hints and tips about what to do.

www.tiggywinkles.com

Orchard Books supports Tiggywinkles.

Registered Charity No. 286447 Tiggywinkles,
Aston Road, Haddenham, Aylesbury,
Buckinghamshire HP17 8AF UK
Tel: 01844 292292
Email: mail@sttiggywinkles.org.uk

Magic
Animal Friends
Can you keep the secret?